# Under
# ONE ROOF

by Alma Flor Ada
illustrated by Nancy Davis

Harcourt

Orlando   Boston   Dallas   Chicago   San Diego

Visit *The Learning Site!*

www.harcourtschool.com

I was so excited when my mother told me that my cousin Bian would be moving to the United States! Bian lives in Vietnam, and she and I are the same age. I hadn't seen Bian for three years, but we had written to each other a lot.

Bian, her younger brother Chim, and their parents would be staying with us until they found a house.

Bian was born in Vietnam. She had been to the United States only once, when she was a baby. I knew things here were going to seem really different to her. When I visited her in Vietnam three years ago, everything over there seemed very different to me.

Bian would have to get used to many new things. The biggest problem she'd have would be learning to speak English. It's hard to make friends when you don't speak the language. However, Bian is so nice that I knew she'd make friends quickly.

I was born in the United States. I speak both English and Vietnamese. My parents were born and raised in Vietnam. I know it was hard for them when they first came here.

They asked me to help Bian fit in. I couldn't wait. I said I'd be glad to introduce her to my friends. I had already told them all about her.

At the airport, I watched Bian's plane land. As soon as we saw each other, we ran to share a big hug. My mother was surprised that Bian wasn't tired after that long flight from Vietnam. My Aunt Hoa and Uncle Gan were very tired. So was Chim.

I would be sharing my room with Bian. My older brother George would be sharing his room with Chim. I was glad I would have someone to talk to and laugh with. Bian always told funny stories.

Bian was nervous and excited about her first day in an American school. I was glad we would be in the same class so I could help her understand everything.

At lunchtime, I introduced Bian to my friends Rosa, Josie, and Jane. I had to translate most of the conversation because Bian spoke very little English. She had studied it for only a few months in Vietnam.

We had tacos for lunch that day. Bian had never seen tacos before. It was funny to see her try to eat them. She kept breaking the taco shells, which made the filling fall out. We all giggled. Bian laughed the hardest.

Rosa showed Bian how to eat tacos. She said, "Hold them this way so the filling won't fall out." Bian tried again, and this time she ate the whole taco without spilling a bit.

As soon as Bian and I got home from school, she told her parents about the tacos. Uncle Gan asked what tacos were. I described them, and Bian told him, "Tacos are very good, but they're tricky to eat!"

We went to my room to do our homework. Bian had a hard time because she couldn't understand the instructions. I helped her and told her to give herself time to learn. "I know it's hard, but you'll learn soon," I said.

The next day at school, Bian kept asking me questions. I tried to help her, but I had to pay attention, too. I told her that it wouldn't be good if we both missed what the teacher was saying. Bian seemed to get a little upset.

At lunchtime she was quiet. I asked her what was wrong, and she said "Nothing." I wondered if she might be homesick.

When Bian and I got home from school, she went into my room and shut the door. I wanted to go in to get my pencil, but my mother asked me to give Bian some time alone. She told me to ask George for a pencil.

When I went into George's room, Chim said George wasn't home. Chim was using George's pencil and he didn't know where any other pencils were. I decided to help Mom and Dad in the kitchen. Finally, Bian came out of my room.

I asked Bian what was wrong. She said she was feeling a little homesick. She really missed her friends. I told her that she would meet new friends soon.

Bian showed me her pictures from home. We spent a long time looking at them. She told me something about each of her friends, and I started to feel as if I knew them. They all seemed so nice. No wonder she missed them so much.

In class, I was assigned to give a speech about volcanoes. I would have to do a lot of research to find the information I needed. I decided to go to the library to find books about volcanoes and start reading about them that night.

When I saw Bian later that day, she told me that she'd been asked to join the school band. She plays the flute very well. She was very happy, even though she would have to practice a lot.

That evening, Bian told her parents the good news about the school band. Chim had good news, too—he had made the soccer team. My cousins were beginning to fit in.

I was happy for them until I tried to start my homework. I couldn't work in my room because Bian was practicing her flute there. I couldn't work in George's room because he and his friends were studying there. I couldn't work downstairs because all the adults were there. I couldn't even work on the back porch because Chim was kicking a soccer ball around the yard. I was so frustrated!

I went to my mother and asked, "When are they moving out?" She asked me why I was upset. I told her it was because I couldn't find a place to work on my speech, and I wanted to do well. Mom invited me to work on it in the kitchen and told me not to worry. "You have a whole week to finish it," she said.

I missed having my own room to study in. The house had been so quiet before my relatives arrived!

When Aunt Hoa and Uncle Gan bought a house, we were all glad. I was happy that I was going to have my room back.

Bian and I had a long talk. We agreed that although we enjoyed being together, we each needed our own space. Her new house would be good for both of us! At the end of our conversation, we were laughing again.

Since Bian and her family moved into their new house, our house seems so empty. I'm glad to have my own room back, but I miss Bian. Of course I see her at school every day still, and we visit each other a lot. Her house is very close to mine.

Today Bian called me to thank me for helping her fit in here. She has met some new friends, and she's learning English very quickly. I'm so glad that she's happy here. I knew she would be!